to Janet and Paul Reynolds
whose table brings family and friends together.

Library of Congress Cataloging-in-Publication Data Available

ISBN 978-1-338-57232-2

10 9 8 7 6 5 4 3 2 1   21 22 23 24 25

Printed in China   62
First edition, October 2021
The text type and display are hand-lettered by Peter H. Reynolds.
Reynolds Studio assistance by Julia Anne Young
Book design by Patti Ann Harris

Our Table

Peter H. Reynolds

ORCHARD BOOKS
AN IMPRINT of SCHOLASTIC INC.

Violet fondly
remembered the table.

She remembered...

...gathering food,

...preparing the table,

...cooking meals,

...lighting candles.

So many stories.
Laughter, singing, celebrating, sharing.
Making memories together.

Recently, though,
Violet found herself
alone at the table.
Her family had become busy.
Very busy.

They had found
new places to be.

Violet found her father
in his favorite chair...
in front of a big screen –
bigger than Violet.

She found her mother
on the staircase…
chatting silently on her phone.

Violet found her brother in his room...
playing games with friends she could not see.

Feeling quite alone,
Violet dreamed of
a time when
family and friends
would gather at the table.

Walking by the room
where their quiet table stood,
Violet did a double-take.

She noticed
something had changed.

Their table was smaller!

The next day,
it had become *even smaller.*

By the end of the week,
the table had shrunk
so much that it fit
easily into the palm
of her hand.

Violet blinked.

The table vanished.

Violet knew exactly
what she had to do.

She asked her father to watch
a show about carpentry together.

And they did.

Violet asked her mother to write
a message and post it
to see who knew
how to build a table.

And they did.

She asked her brother
to use his computer
to help draw out a plan together.

And they did.

Violet was ready.

She asked her family
to build a table — together.

And... they did.

When they were done,
Violet paused to marvel
at their creation.

A place to come together,
to share stories once again.

A table to
make memories.

A table stronger,
more beautiful than ever.

And... it was.